DINK, JOSH, AND RUTH ROSE
AREN'T THE ONLY KID DETECTIVES!

WHAT ABOUT YOU?

CAN YOU FIND THE HIDDEN MESSAGE INSIDE THIS BOOK?

There are 26 illustrations in this book, not counting the one on the title page, the map at the beginning, and the picture of the coin box that repeats at the start of many of the chapters. In each of the 26 illustrations, there's a hidden letter. If you can find all the letters, you will spell out a secret message!

If you're stumped, the answer is on the bottom of page 133.

HAPPY DETECTING!

This book is dedicated to the memory
of Dr. Michael Pardue.
—R.R.

To Raymond
—J.S.G.

Visit us on the Web!
SteppingStonesBooks.com
randomhousekids.com

Educators and librarians, for a variety of teaching tools,
visit us at RHTeachersLibrarians.com

Library of Congress Cataloging-in-Publication Data is available upon request.
ISBN 978-0-399-55195-6 (trade) — ISBN 978-0-399-55196-3 (lib. bdg.) —
ISBN 978-0-399-55197-0 (ebook)

Printed in the United States of America
10 9 8 7 6 5 4 3 2 1

This book has been officially leveled by using the F&P Text Level Gradient™ Leveling System.

A to Z Mysteries®

SUPER EDITION 9

APRIL FOOLS' FIASCO

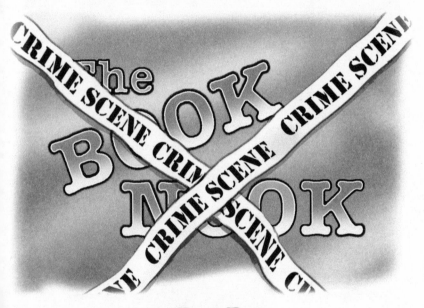

by Ron Roy

illustrated by
John Steven Gurney

A STEPPING STONE BOOK™

Random House 🏠 New York

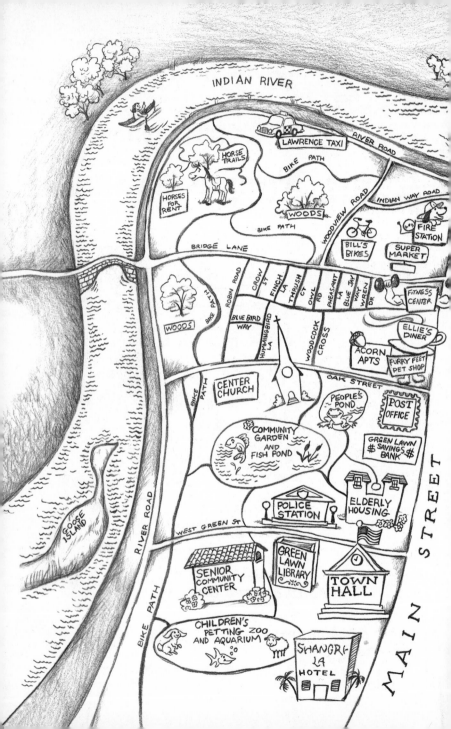

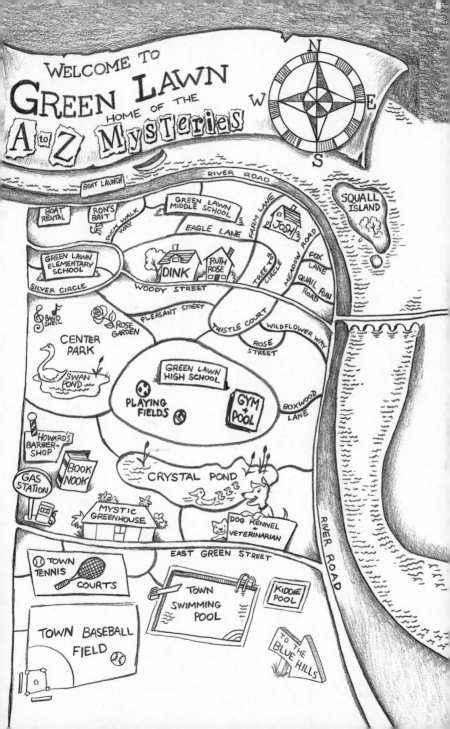

CHAPTER 1

"Why does it have to rain?" Josh asked as he and his friends left the playing fields. "How can I practice my soccer skills in the mud?"

"It's not raining yet," Dink said, looking up at the dark clouds. "Besides, real soccer players aren't afraid of getting wet."

Josh passed his soccer ball to Dink, who kicked it to Ruth Rose. The three had been playing soccer after school on a Friday afternoon.

Dink's full name was Donald David

Duncan. He, Josh Pinto, and Ruth Rose Hathaway were fourth graders and best friends.

"We need the rain in April," Ruth Rose told Josh. "That's what makes the flowers bloom in May!"

Ruth Rose liked to wear outfits all the same color. Today's choice was bright yellow, like the daffodils that grew outside their school building.

She passed the ball back to Josh. "Let's stop at the Book Nook," she said. "I heard Wallis Wallace has a new book out. Maybe Mr. Paskey has it."

Wallis Wallace was a famous children's book author. She and Dink, Josh, and Ruth Rose had been friends ever since the kids had tried to save her from a kidnapper. The kidnapping turned out to be fake, but they stayed friends anyway.

Josh slapped the pockets of his cargo

pants. He heard a few coins jingle. "I don't have enough money to buy a book," he said.

Dink shoved his hand into his jeans pocket. "I've got exactly one quarter," he said.

"I just got my allowance," Ruth Rose said. "If Wallis Wallace's new book is there, I'll buy it and you can both read it when I'm done."

When they passed Howard's Barbershop, they waved at Howard through the window. He smiled and waved back.

Outside the Book Nook, a woman with a backpack slung over one shoulder was standing near the door. Dink noticed a small yellow smiley face pinned to one of the pack's straps.

She was reading a flyer taped inside the window. When she walked through the door, the kids stopped to read the flyer:

CALLING ALL NUMISMATISTS!

COME TO THE NUMISMATIC SOCIETY MEETING!

WEST HARTFORD LIBRARY, MAIN STREET

APRIL 2, 10:00–4:00

SELL OR TRADE YOUR OLD COINS

AND BILLS! FREE REFRESHMENTS!

Under the words was a drawing of a jar of coins and a stack of green bills.

"What's a numis . . . whatever?" Josh asked.

Ruth Rose pointed to the drawing. "Something about money, I think," she said.

"Cool!" said Josh. "I love money! And free food, too. We should go to the meeting!"

Dink, Josh, and Ruth Rose stepped inside the Book Nook. Mr. Paskey was helping a bald man with blue sneakers pick out a book. He smiled and waved at them.

The kids walked to the children's section. They passed a man in a red shirt, stacking boxes of new books in a corner. When he was finished, he waved to Mr. Paskey and left the store.

Near the children's area, Dink noticed a trapdoor leading to the basement. He heard someone down there whistling and making clanking noises.

"Here it is!" Ruth Rose cried, grabbing

a book off a shelf. She turned it over and looked at a smiling photo of Wallis Wallace.

Ruth Rose held the book so Dink and Josh could see the cover. It was called *The Dark Forest.* The cover showed a boy and girl surrounded by tall, dark trees. Vines that looked like a sea creature's tentacles were wrapped around the tree trunks. Evil-looking birds sat in the branches, their red eyes glaring.

"That's pretty scary," Josh said. "Those eyes give me goose bumps!"

"Great, I'll buy it," Ruth Rose said. "We can do rock, paper, scissors to see who reads it first."

"No, you read it first," Dink said. "Then give it to Josh. I want to count his goose bumps!"

The bald man left the store, and Mr. Paskey met the kids at the counter. "Ah, I see you found Ms. Wallace's new book," he said. "I read it, and I got goose bumps!"

"See?" Josh said.

"That's why I want to buy it," Ruth Rose said. "I love scary stories."

Dink noticed two stacks of flyers on the counter. One stack had the flyer they'd seen in the window. The other flyers were red, white, and blue. They showed a drawing of a big brick house and a photo of a man with white hair and a big mustache.

Dink read the words beneath the man's face:

JOIN US AT THE MARK TWAIN HOUSE
APRIL 3 FROM 6 TO 10 P.M.!
COME CELEBRATE MARK TWAIN'S LIFE!
FOOD, MUSIC, BALLOONS FOR THE KIDS!
351 FARMINGTON AVENUE, HARTFORD, CT

"Your dad is a Mark Twain fan, isn't he?" Mr. Paskey asked Dink.

Dink nodded. "I think so," he said.

Mr. Paskey handed him a flyer. "Take this home for him," he said. "He may want to attend the party."

Dink slipped the flyer into his pocket.

While Ruth Rose paid Mr. Paskey for the book, Josh picked up a flyer like the one in the window. "What's this about?" he asked Mr. Paskey.

"Oh, every year the Numismatic Society has a big meeting," Mr. Paskey said. "People who like to collect old coins and other forms of money get together."

"Cool!" said Josh, putting the flyer in his pocket. "What do they do?"

"Well, they swap with each other or sell to the public," Mr. Paskey answered. "If you're a coin collector, like me, you'd go there to meet other coin collectors."

In the mirror behind Mr. Paskey's counter, Dink saw the reflection of a woman approaching the counter. She was wearing jeans and a gray shirt with

DALE PLUMBING stitched over the pocket, and she was holding a toolbox. Her hands had black smudges, and her face was sweaty. "I fixed the leak," she told Mr. Paskey. "Your basement floor got a bit wet, so I mopped it for you. Mind if I wash up in your bathroom?"

"Of course, Amanda," Mr. Paskey said.

Amanda set her toolbox on the floor and walked toward the bathroom.

Mr. Paskey pulled a small blue book from a drawer under the counter and handed it to Josh. The book looked as if it had been read a lot. "This is about coin collecting," he said. "Take it home and give it a read. We might turn you into a numismatist!"

"What is a nu . . . what you said?" Josh asked.

"Numismatists collect and study money," Mr. Paskey explained.

"Cool!" Josh said. "I definitely want

to be one, but I can't even say it!"

"Break the word into four syllables," Mr. Paskey said. "Noo-MIZ-muh-tist."

Josh repeated, "Noo-MIZ-muh-tist."

Something caught Dink's eye, and he looked up into the mirror again. He thought he saw a moving shadow behind him, between two rows of bookshelves. When he turned around to get a

better look, the shadow was gone.

Dink glanced out the window, thinking he might have seen a reflection of someone walking by the store. But the sidewalk in front of the Book Nook was empty.

Amanda came out of the bathroom. Her face and hands were clean. "Thanks a lot, Mr. Paskey," she said. "I feel a hundred percent better!"

Mr. Paskey took a key from a hook next to the cash register. He walked Amanda to the door, locked it behind her, and pulled a shade down over the glass.

"I want to show you kids something," Mr. Paskey said, putting the key back on the hook. He winked at Josh. "For numismatists only!"

CHAPTER 2

On a shelf behind the cash register, a glass case stood under the mirror. Inside, the kids could see some old-looking coins and a wooden box.

Mr. Paskey took a small key from his pocket and unlocked the case. He slid the box out and set it on the counter. It was about twelve inches long on each side and four inches high. Carvings of elephants, vines, and flowers decorated the wood.

"That's such a beautiful box!" Ruth Rose said. "Did you make it?"

"No, my grandfather did, about forty years ago," Mr. Paskey said. "Granddad Paskey gave it to me on my tenth birthday. I used to hide my treasures in it. Now it's where I keep my coin collection."

"You collect coins?" Josh asked. "So are you one of those noo-MIZ . . . ?"

"Yes, I'm a numismatist," Mr. Paskey said. "I started with a few coins when I was your age. Now I have hundreds."

"Why do people collect coins?" Josh asked. "I like to spend them!"

"People collect for lots of reasons," Mr. Paskey said. "Some collectors just like to look at the coins. They can be quite beautiful. Others do it for the money they can get if they sell their coins."

He took the blue book from Josh's hand and flipped through the pages. Then he put his finger on a picture of an old nickel. "This 1913 Liberty Head nickel is very valuable," he said. "There were only five minted, so they're extremely rare. One just like this sold for around three million dollars!"

"THREE MILLION!" Josh squawked. "For one nickel? Why?"

"You can read all about it later in the book," Mr. Paskey said. He turned more pages until he came to another picture. "See these quarters? Some of them are worth thousands of dollars."

He passed the book back to Josh. "Whenever you get a quarter, check to see if it looks like one of those," he said. "Do you kids have any coins today?"

The kids quickly emptied their pockets. Ruth Rose had a wallet holding five one-dollar bills and $2.47 in change.

Josh had seventy-seven cents: two quarters, two dimes, one nickel, and two pennies.

Dink pulled a quarter from his pocket.

With the kids watching, Mr. Paskey looked at each coin through a small, round glass he held up to one eye.

"What's that thing?" Dink asked.

"It's called a loupe," Mr. Paskey told him. "It makes things look bigger."

"Is any of our money worth a million dollars?" Dink asked.

Mr. Paskey smiled. "Nope. Your quarter is worth exactly twenty-five cents, Dink. Sorry!"

Josh opened the book and studied the pictures of the coins. "Well, now I want to be an artist *and* a noo-MIZ-muh-tist," he said.

"That's wonderful, Josh!" Mr. Paskey said. "If you have time, try to go to the meeting tomorrow."

"Maybe I will," Josh said. "I love money almost as much as I love ice cream!"

Mr. Paskey's face changed from happy to sad. "Speaking of ice cream, I have some bad news," he said. "Ellie is closing her diner."

CHAPTER 3

"OH NO!" Ruth Rose yelled.

"Green Lawn won't be the same without Ellie's Diner!" Dink said. "Why is she closing?"

Mr. Paskey shook his head. "Ellie found out she's allergic to ice cream," he said.

"What? No way!" Josh yelped.

"Yes way," Mr. Paskey said. "Ellie's very upset. You should go say good-bye before she closes forever!"

Dink, Josh, and Ruth Rose dashed

out of the Book Nook. They raced to the crossing light in front of the Green Lawn Savings Bank. When the light said WALK, they hurried up Main Street to the diner.

It started to rain as they burst through the door. Ellie was hanging up the phone. She had a funny look on her face.

"Hi, kids," Ellie said. The corners of her mouth were turned down. Her eyes looked sad.

"Mr. Paskey told us you were closing!" Josh cried.

"You can't close the diner!" Ruth Rose said. "We need you!"

"Are you really allergic to ice cream?" Dink asked.

Ellie put her head down. She covered her face with her hands. Her shoulders started to shake.

The kids looked at each other. They didn't know what to do. Ellie was crying!

Then Ellie looked up with a grin on

her face. "April Fools!" she cried. "Mr. Paskey just called and told me what he said to you! I'm not closing my diner— he was just playing a trick on you!"

Josh put his hand over his heart. "Oh my gosh, I was getting ready to faint!" he said.

Ellie laughed. "No fainting allowed," she said. "And to make up for the trick, free cones for you three!"

The kids put their noses close to the display case to see all the flavors. Dink asked for chocolate, Josh picked pistachio, and Ruth Rose chose lemon, to match her yellow outfit.

They took their cones to a booth where they had a view of the park across the street.

"I forgot today was April first," Dink said after taking a lick of his ice cream. "Mr. Paskey sure fooled us!"

Josh took a big slurp off the top of

his pistachio. "I don't think it's very nice for grown-ups to play tricks on kids," he said.

Ruth Rose laughed. "Joshua Pinto, how can you say that?" she asked. "Do you remember when you tricked the twins into thinking your pony was talking to them, telling them to do your chores?"

Josh giggled. "That was awesome," he said. "I hid in Polly's stall behind some hay. When Brian and Bradley came in to feed her, I made a pony voice and they thought Polly was talking! 'MAKE JOSH'S BED!' I told them."

"So what's the difference between you tricking your little brothers and Mr. Paskey tricking us?" Dink asked.

"Simple," Josh said. "People expect kids to play tricks. But adults . . ." Josh got a sly look on his face. "Dink, you just gave me a brilliant idea!"

"Uh-oh," Dink muttered. "I'm afraid to ask, but I will. What's your *brilliant* idea?"

Josh leaned in and whispered, "I'm going to play an April Fools' trick on Mr. Paskey!" He grinned from behind his cone.

"What kind of trick?" asked Ruth Rose. "Mr. Paskey is real smart. You won't be able to fool him like you did your little brothers."

Josh tapped his forehead. "I'll think of something," he said. "Mr. Paskey may be smart, but not as smart as my megabrain!"

Dink and Ruth Rose laughed. They finished their cones as they watched raindrops streak the window.

Dink picked up the blue book Mr. Paskey had given to Josh. He flipped a few pages. "Look, here's that nickel Mr. Paskey told us about," he said.

"This tells how some rich guy bought it from another rich guy for three million dollars!"

Josh gazed out the window. "I wonder what I'd do with three million dollars," he said.

"Buy ice cream?" Ruth Rose teased. "For your two best friends?"

Josh grinned. "Maybe," he said. "And maybe not."

Dink looked at the page again. "This says there are only five of those nickels in the world, and three are in museums."

"Where are the other two?" asked Ruth Rose.

"Two rich coin collectors own them," Dink said. "Hey, one of those numismatist guys lives in Connecticut!"

"Dink, you just gave me my second brilliant idea of the day!" Josh said. "The perfect trick to play on Mr. Paskey!"

CHAPTER 4

"Tell us!" Ruth Rose said.

"Okay," Josh said. "Mr. Paskey owns a bookstore, right? And kids buy books there, right?"

"Josh, we know that," Dink said. "Tell us your trick!"

Just then a skinny guy came in. He wore a baseball cap that partly covered his face. The guy stopped at the counter and wiped raindrops from his glasses while he glanced at the ice cream choices.

Josh grinned. "Okay, here's the plan,"

he said. "I'm going to tell Mr. Paskey that some kid came into his store to buy a book. The kid paid for the book with a bunch of coins he had in his pocket. One of the coins was a nickel like the one in this book, worth three million dollars!"

Dink and Ruth Rose just looked at him.

"How is that going to work?" Ruth Rose asked. "Mr. Paskey knows that two of those nickels are owned by rich collectors. The other three are locked up in museums. So how does a kid have one?"

"I'm getting to that part," Josh said. "That's why my idea is so—"

"Brilliant?" Dink asked.

"Yes!"

The skinny man brought his cup of ice cream to the booth behind the kids. He pulled out a cell phone, typed a number, and began talking. Dink heard

him say, "Mark's party" and something
about a cake.

"What's your brilliant idea?" Ruth
Rose asked Josh.

"Be prepared to be amazed," Josh
said. He leaned closer to Dink and Ruth
Rose. "My grandfather plays a game
with us every time my brothers and I
visit him. He hides money, and if we
find it, we get to keep it."

"That sounds like a great game,"
Dink said. "But I didn't know your
grandfather was rich."

"He isn't," Josh said. "He just hides
nickels and dimes."

"Okay, but what does your grandfather have to do with Mr. Paskey?"
Ruth Rose asked.

"I'm not finished," Josh said. "I'm
going to tell Mr. Paskey that one of the
two collectors who own those nickels

plays that game with *his* grandson. He hides money, and his grandson gets to keep what he finds."

"Don't tell me!" Dink cried. "The grandson found—"

"Yes!" Josh said. "The grandson accidentally found that valuable nickel and put it in his pocket."

"And then he spent it in Mr. Paskey's store?" asked Ruth Rose.

Josh nodded, looking like a sly fox.

"But how did this kid find the coin?" Dink asked. "I mean, if it's so valuable, wouldn't his grandfather keep it locked in a safe?"

Josh thought for a minute. Then he tapped his forehead and grinned. "Here's what happened," he said. "The rich guy was at his desk, messing around with some of his most valuable coins, when he heard the doorbell. So he picked up the coins, then shoved them into a drawer and went to answer the door."

Josh grinned again. "But he missed one nickel on his desk," he said. "When he opened the door, it was his grandson. Granddad went to the kitchen for some milk and cookies while the kid wandered around the house looking for hidden coins. He saw the rare nickel and put it in his pocket, not knowing it was part of his grandfather's collection."

"He thought his grandfather left the nickel on the desk for him to find, like in the game?" Ruth Rose asked.

"Right," Josh said.

"Okay, the kid got the coin," Dink said, "but how did he spend it in the Book Nook?"

Josh squinted his eyes. "The kid lives in Hartford," he said. "His mom drives him to Green Lawn, and they walk into the Book Nook. The kid has the nickel in his pocket, along with his allowance. He buys a book, and Mr. Paskey puts the money in his cash register."

Dink blinked. "You mean this kid spent a three-million-dollar nickel to buy some three-dollar book?" he asked.

Josh nodded and grinned. "Yep."

CHAPTER 5

Ruth Rose looked at Dink. "It *is* kind of brilliant," she said.

Just then the guy in the baseball cap jumped up from his seat and ran out of the diner.

"So what happens after you tell Mr. Paskey this crazy story?" Dink asked Josh.

"Then Mr. Paskey rushes to his cash register and starts looking at all his nickels through that *loopy* thing," Josh said.

"It's a loupe," Ruth Rose said. "My

uncle uses one when he examines his stamp collection."

"But won't Mr. Paskey wonder how you, Josh Pinto, know about this kid and his grandfather?" Dink asked Josh.

Josh pointed to the small TV on the wall behind Ellie's counter. "He probably won't ask, but if he does, I'll tell him I saw it on TV. Big news story!"

Ellie came by with a wet sponge. "How was your ice cream?" she asked.

"It was delicious, thank you," said Dink.

Ellie wiped the empty table behind theirs. "Oh, that guy who was just here forgot his glasses," she said. "He didn't even finish his marshmallow fudge nut ice cream!" She picked up the glasses and hurried out the door after him.

"So when are you going to pull this

brilliant trick on poor Mr. Paskey?" Dink asked.

"Tomorrow," Josh said, working on his cone.

"But April Fools' Day is *today*," Ruth Rose said.

"That's why this is going to be so awesome," Josh said. "If I go back to the Book Nook today and tell him a kid spent a three-million-dollar nickel in his store, he'll know I'm just goofing on him."

Josh tapped his forehead. "But if I spring this on him tomorrow, when it *isn't* April Fools' Day, he'll never expect a trick. It'll be perfect!"

The next morning, Dink, Josh, and Ruth Rose met and walked to the Book Nook. Josh was mumbling to himself, rehearsing the story he planned to tell Mr. Paskey.

Suddenly they heard a siren, and a police cruiser raced past them. It was headed down Main Street, in the same direction they were going.

"Come on!" Josh said, and the kids took off after the cruiser.

Five minutes later, they reached the Book Nook, out of breath. Mr. Paskey was standing out front, talking to Officer Fallon, Green Lawn's chief of police. His cruiser was parked in front of the store.

"I wonder what's going on," Josh said.

"Officer Fallon is here to arrest you," Dink whispered.

"For what?" Josh asked.

"For lying to Mr. Paskey."

Ruth Rose giggled. "Twenty years in jail for Josh," she said.

"No way," Josh said. "I won't be lying, just April-fooling him."

Officer Fallon noticed the kids. "Hi, gang," he said. "What's going on?"

"Um, we're just here to see Mr. Paskey," Dink said. "Josh has something to tell him."

"Well, I hope you can cheer him up," Officer Fallon said.

Mr. Paskey turned around. His face was pale, and he looked as if he hadn't slept in a week. His hair was mussed, and Mr. Paskey *always* combed his hair.

"Mr. Paskey, what's wrong?" Dink asked.

"Someone broke into my store last night," Mr. Paskey said. He sounded as if he had a sore throat.

"You're kidding!" Josh said.

"Did they take anything?" Ruth Rose asked.

Mr. Paskey swallowed, then said, "They stole my coin collection and my grandfather's box!"

"That's awful!" Ruth Rose said.

Just then Officer Keene came around the corner of the Book Nook. "No sign of forced entry anywhere," he said.

"Okay, let's go inside," Officer Fallon said. "I want to see the damage and those footprints you told me about."

Mr. Paskey led the two officers inside, with the kids following. He stopped and pointed. One side of his glass display case was shattered. Sharp pieces of glass were scattered across the counter and the floor.

The coins and the carved box were gone.

Someone had spray-painted HA! HA! HA! across the case's door in yellow letters.

CHAPTER 6

They all stared at the smashed case. Officer Fallon touched one of the sprayed letters. "The paint is dry," he said. "Must've been done hours ago."

"But who would do this?" Mr. Paskey asked.

"Maybe it's supposed to be some April Fools' joke," Dink said.

"But it's not a joke!" Mr. Paskey wailed. "My coins are gone, and my grandfather's box!"

"You're right," Officer Keene said. "This is no joke. It's grand theft! And spraying HA! HA! HA! means the crook is laughing at you!"

Dink didn't know what to say. He looked at Mr. Paskey, who had tears in his eyes.

Officer Fallon put his hand on Mr. Paskey's shoulder. "Come on," he said. "Show me the footprints."

They walked to the bathroom in the rear of the store. Mr. Paskey shoved the door open wider. "There," he said. "Damp footprints on the floor and on the toilet seat."

He pointed to the small window next to the toilet. "And I found that window open," he said. "When I left last night, it was closed and locked."

Officer Keene bent down and studied the dirty footprints. "Made by medium-size feet," he said, placing his own large shoe next to one of the prints.

"I don't see how anyone could get

through that window," Officer Fallon said, "if it really was locked."

"It was," Mr. Paskey said.

"Who uses this bathroom during the day?" Officer Keene asked.

"I do," Mr. Paskey said. "Sometimes a customer will ask, but not often."

"Yesterday you let the plumber wash her hands in here," Dink said.

"You're right. I forgot about that," Mr. Paskey said. "Her hands were dirty because she'd fixed a leak in my basement."

"So maybe these are the plumber's footprints," Officer Fallon said.

Mr. Paskey shook his head. "No, I'm pretty sure this floor was clean when I went home," he said. "I check the bathroom every night before I leave."

"Then we've got a real mystery on our hands," Officer Fallon said. "You say nobody was in the store when you closed up, yet somebody left these footprints here!"

Officer Keene touched one of the footprints, then looked at what his finger had picked up. "It's not dirt from a yard or garden," he said. "It's more gritty, like tiny pieces of stone or cement."

"Mr. Paskey, are you absolutely, one hundred percent sure this floor was clean when you locked up and went home?" Officer Fallon asked.

Mr. Paskey closed his eyes for a moment. "Well, maybe not one hundred percent sure," he said. "All I know is that I usually check the bathroom every night. I suppose I could have forgotten."

"And who was the last person in here?" Officer Keene asked.

"Amanda Dale, the plumber," Mr. Paskey said.

"And before coming in here, she had been in your basement fixing a leak, right?" Officer Keene went on.

Mr. Paskey nodded.

"So she probably had wet, gritty stuff on her feet when she came out of the basement and walked into this bathroom, right?" Officer Keene continued. "Leaving tracks on your bathroom floor."

"Yes, I guess she could have," said Mr. Paskey. "But as I told you, the floor was clean when I went home. If Amanda came in here with dirty shoes, she cleaned up after herself."

"How well do you know Amanda?" Officer Fallon asked Mr. Paskey.

"Pretty well," Mr. Paskey said. "Her father, Steve Dale, used to be my plumber. When he retired last year, Amanda took over his business."

"Think real hard," Officer Fallon said to Mr. Paskey. "Would Amanda have any reason to unlock this window while she was in here washing her hands?"

"I don't see why she would," Mr. Paskey said. "But she might have, I suppose."

"It happened on April Fools' Day," Officer Keene pointed out. "Could this plumber—Amanda—be playing a prank?"

"Some plumbers carry spray paint in their toolboxes," Officer Fallon said. "They use it to mark pipes where they want to cut."

Mr. Paskey shook his head. "She'd never do that. Her dad and I have been friends for years," he said. "We collect coins together. Amanda knows how important our collections are."

Officer Fallon looked at Officer Keene. "Maybe we'd better talk to Amanda Dale anyway," he said quietly.

They all walked back toward the front of the store.

"I'm sorry for your trouble, Mr. Paskey," Officer Fallon said. "I'd like you to make a list of everyone who came into your store in the last couple of days."

"But I don't remember everyone," Mr. Paskey said. Then he added, "Do you think the thief was one of my customers?"

"It had to be someone who knew about those coins," Officer Fallon said. "Just do the best you can with the list."

The officers started to leave. Officer Keene stopped and turned around. "Would you have Ms. Dale's phone number?" he asked.

"Yes," Mr. Paskey said. He pulled a business card from a drawer and handed it to Officer Keene. "You won't tell Amanda that I'm accusing her of anything, will you? Because I'm not."

"We just want to ask a few questions," Officer Fallon said. "Maybe get her fingerprints. So please don't touch that bathroom window, in case her prints are there. In fact, I'd like you to lock the bathroom door now. And don't touch the glass case, either. We'll need to check it and the bathroom for fingerprints."

The two officers left. Dink watched

them climb into their cruiser and pull away up Main Street.

While Mr. Paskey was locking the bathroom door, Josh pulled Dink and Ruth Rose behind a bookshelf. "Should I tell him you-know-what?" he whispered. "It might cheer him up, like Officer Fallon said."

"You mean the story about the boy and the nickel?" Ruth Rose asked.

Josh nodded.

"I think you should," Dink said. "But tell him it was meant to be an April Fools' joke."

CHAPTER 7

Mr. Paskey walked over to the counter. He still looked pretty upset, but his hair was combed. "Now, what can I do for you kids today?" he asked. "Need more copies of *The Dark Forest*?"

"No, but I want to tell you something," Josh said. "It's sort of a joke." His face turned pink.

"Good, I can use a joke," Mr. Paskey said, glancing around. "I still can't believe my coins are gone!"

Josh explained the trick he had been planning to pull on him. When he was finished, all three kids stared at Mr. Paskey.

Is he going to be upset at us? Dink wondered.

Mr. Paskey grinned. "That's brilliant!" he said. "I would have checked all the nickels in the store, then run to the bank to look over last night's deposit. That would have been a terrific April Fools' trick, Josh. How did you think of something so clever?"

"I got the idea from that coin book you gave me," Josh said.

Mr. Paskey looked at the broken glass case. "Well, I'd better start on that list," he sighed.

The kids left the Book Nook. Through the window, they could see Mr. Paskey writing on a pad.

"I feel so bad for him," Ruth Rose said.

"Me too," Josh said.

"I just can't believe the crook is someone Mr. Paskey knows," Ruth Rose

The BOOK NOOK

said. "Like a customer or that plumber."

"I know," Dink said, thinking about the HA! HA! HA! sprayed on the glass case. "I'll bet it was a stranger."

It began to rain again. Dink put up the hood on his sweatshirt. "I have money today," he said. "From *my* coin collection. I'll treat for hot chocolates at Ellie's."

The kids hurried up Main Street.

The booths in Ellie's Diner were all taken because it was a rainy Saturday.

Ellie was bustling between the counter and the booths, waiting on people.

"Gee, maybe I could work here," Josh said. "I could be an ice cream scooper!"

"You mean an ice cream *eater*," Dink said. "Ellie would never let you near her ice cream!"

The kids sat at the counter and ordered three hot chocolates.

"We should tell Ellie about Mr. Paskey's coin collection," Ruth Rose said.

"She's pretty busy," Dink said. "Besides, Mr. Paskey will probably tell her himself."

They sipped their hot chocolates and watched Ellie zooming around the diner, helping her customers.

"Officer Fallon thinks it was her," Josh said.

"Who?" Dink asked. "Ellie?"

"No, *Amanda*," Josh said.

"I don't see how she could have

done it," Dink said. "We saw her leave the Book Nook after she came out of the bathroom."

"But Officer Fallon thinks she might have unlocked the bathroom window," Josh said. "Maybe she came back after the store was closed and climbed through it with dirty feet."

"So you think those were *her* footprints?" Ruth Rose asked.

"It makes sense," Josh said.

The three kids sipped and thought about Amanda Dale stealing Mr. Paskey's coins.

"Well, if it was Amanda, maybe Officer Fallon will find her fingerprints on the window and the lock," Dink said.

"But she could just say she wanted some fresh air, so she opened the window," Ruth Rose said. "Her fingerprints on the window don't prove she took the coins."

"Unless she also left fingerprints on the glass case while she was spraying HA! HA! HA!" Josh said. "She'd have a hard time explaining that!"

"Guys, I don't think it was Amanda," Dink said. "Mr. Paskey knows her, and he trusts her." He sighed. "But some burglar got inside the Book Nook and stole those coins!"

After a minute, Josh said, "Maybe not."

"What do you mean?" Ruth Rose asked.

"Maybe there was no burglar at all," Josh said. "What if Mr. Paskey made those footprints to fool us? What if he just took his coin collection home?"

"Why would he do that?" Dink asked.

Josh smiled. "To play another big, fat April Fools' joke on us!"

CHAPTER 8

Dink and Ruth Rose stared at Josh.

"You think Mr. Paskey made the whole thing up as a trick?" Dink asked.

Josh shrugged. "I'm just saying," he said.

"Well, I don't," Ruth Rose said. "Mr. Paskey would never play that kind of trick on Officer Fallon and Officer Keene."

"But what if they were in on it *with* Mr. Paskey?" Josh said. "We know Ellie was in on the first trick he played on us."

Dink shook his head. "No, I don't buy it," he said. "Did you see Mr. Paskey's face when he showed us the smashed case? That was real!"

"And he'd never wreck his own glass case just to play a trick," Ruth Rose added.

"Then it must have been a burglar," Josh said. "But how did he get into the store?"

"You just gave me an idea," Dink told Josh.

"Not me," Josh said. "I never give ideas away for free!"

"What's your idea, Dink?" Ruth Rose asked.

"We've been trying to figure out how someone got in," Dink said, "but what if the thief was *already* inside? What if he used the window to get *out* of the store, not to get *in*?"

"But who?" Ruth Rose asked.

"There were people in the store when we got there," Josh said. He counted on three fingers: "Amanda was there, plus a bald guy wearing blue sneakers and the delivery guy stacking the boxes. But we saw them all leave the store."

"Josh is right," Ruth Rose said. "And I remember Mr. Paskey locking the door before he showed us his coin box."

Dink shook his head. "*Somebody* left those footprints," he said. "And I don't think it was Amanda."

"Maybe it was a ghost with dirty feet," Josh whispered.

They all stared into the mirror behind Ellie's counter. Dink thought of the mirror behind Mr. Paskey's counter.

"We're missing a piece of this puzzle," he said.

"Well, I just thought of something," Ruth Rose said.

"Tell us," Dink said.

Ruth Rose looked at Josh. "Yesterday, when you told Dink and me about the trick you wanted to play on Mr. Paskey, we were here," she said. "In Ellie's."

Josh nodded. "In that booth." He pointed to a booth near the window. Today the seats were all taken by a bunch of teenagers.

"Other people were here, too," Ruth Rose continued. "So maybe someone overheard your story about the kid who spent a valuable nickel in the Book Nook. What if *that person* is the thief?"

"You mean this *someone* might have thought that stuff I made up was *real*?" Josh asked.

Ruth Rose nodded.

"Oh my gosh, I just remembered!" Dink said. "That guy who came in here yesterday and sat in the booth behind ours was on his cell phone. I heard him talking about a party for someone named Mark."

"That's right. I remember him, too!" Ruth Rose said. "He's the one who forgot his glasses, and Ellie ran out to try to find him."

"What about him?" Josh asked.

"Right after you told us about the fake kid who spent his fake nickel in the Book Nook, he took off real fast!" Dink said.

"So you think he's the thief with muddy feet?" Josh asked.

"It could be him," Dink said. "He was sitting close enough to hear what you said."

"But none of what I said was true!" Josh said. "I was just telling you guys about my joke!"

"*We* know that, Josh," Dink said. "But the guy sitting behind us didn't know it was a joke. He didn't hear everything you said, so to him that stuff about the nickel must have sounded real!"

"But, Dink, you just told us you thought the thief was already inside the

Book Nook," Ruth Rose reminded him.

"I know, but maybe I was wrong," Dink said.

"Then we're back to the same problem," Ruth Rose said. "How could that guy get inside Mr. Paskey's store through a locked bathroom window?"

Ellie came and sat on a stool next to Dink. "I need to hire some help!" she said.

"How about me?" Josh asked. "I'm a super ice cream scooper!"

Ellie winked at Josh. "Ask me again when you turn sixteen, sweetie," she said.

"Ellie, do you remember that man who left his glasses yesterday?" Dink asked.

"Sure, skinny guy wearing a cap.

He was here the other day, asking if he could leave some flyers," Ellie said. "I tried to catch him yesterday when he ran out, but he was already driving away in a snazzy yellow jeep. When he pulled away, I saw a red-white-and-blue bumper sticker with a face on it."

Something clicked for Dink. He pulled the red-white-and-blue flyer from his pocket and spread it on the counter. "Did the bumper sticker look like this?"

Ellie nodded. "Exactly," she said.

They all looked at the picture of the man with white hair and a big mustache.

"He was on the bumper sticker!" Ellie said.

"It's Mark Twain," Dink said. "They're having a party for him this week."

"Who is?" Josh asked.

"This place," Dink said. He put his finger on the drawing of the big brick house. "It's where he lived, in Hartford. The Mark Twain House."

"Oh, I know where that is!" Ruth Rose said. "My parents took me there for Christmas one year. People dressed in old-timey costumes and sang Christmas carols. We drank hot chocolate!"

Ellie went to wait on a new customer.

Dink looked at his friends in the mirror. "The guy who was here yesterday was talking on his cell phone about a party for Mark," he said. "He might have overheard your story about the three-million-dollar nickel and decided to break in and try to find it! When he saw the coins in the case, he smashed it and took the box."

"But, Dink, how did he get into the Book Nook?" Josh asked.

"I thought about that, too," Dink said.

"He could have stolen the door key."

"How?" Josh asked.

"Mr. Paskey keeps his keys on a hook behind the counter," Dink said. "I'm thinking this guy dropped off Mr. Paskey's flyers, too. And while he was in the Book Nook, he could've grabbed the keys when Mr. Paskey wasn't looking!"

"But the keys were still there today," Ruth Rose said. "I saw Mr. Paskey use them."

"I saw him, too," Dink said. "But I'll bet Mr. Paskey has more than one set."

"But, Dink, that guy didn't know about the three-million-dollar nickel until yesterday," Josh said. "Why would he steal the keys days ago, when he left the flyers?"

Dink shrugged. "Who knows?" he said. "Maybe he planned to come in some night to rob the register or steal some books."

"Running out of here after he heard Josh talking about that nickel is pretty suspicious," Ruth Rose said.

"Too bad we don't know this guy's name," Josh said.

"Right, but we *do* know where to find him," Dink said.

"Where?" Josh asked.

Dink tapped the flyer. "At Mark Twain's party tomorrow," he said.

"We need to tell Officer Fallon!" Ruth Rose said.

CHAPTER 9

It was still raining, so the kids ran down Main Street. They cut behind the elderly housing building and sprinted for the police station's back entrance.

Dink stood on a small rug inside the door. "Wipe your feet or they'll arrest you," he whispered.

They wiped their feet, then followed a hallway to Officer Fallon's office. Dink knocked on the door.

"Come in!" Officer Fallon said in his deep voice.

The kids stepped inside. Officer Fallon was sitting at his desk, typing on his computer keyboard. A mug of tea sat on a napkin.

"Well, hello again," Officer Fallon said. "You look damp." He handed the kids some paper towels.

The kids wiped their hair and faces.

"What brings you three to the police station?" the chief asked.

Taking turns, the kids told Officer Fallon about the April Fools' Day trick Josh had been planning for Mr. Paskey. Then they told him about the guy who might have overheard the story in Ellie's.

"He ran out fast," Josh said. "He might have thought Mr. Paskey really *did* have that three-million-dollar nickel in his store."

"He could have come back last night and stolen the coin collection!" Ruth Rose added.

Officer Fallon picked up a pencil and began making notes on a pad. "Can you describe this fellow?" he asked.

"He was pretty young," Dink said. "Maybe twenty. He had on glasses and a baseball cap."

"And he was skinny," Ruth Rose added.

"Ellie saw him drive away in a yellow jeep," Josh said.

Dink showed Officer Fallon the flyer that was like the bumper sticker Ellie had noticed on the guy's car.

"Your thinking is sound," Officer Fallon said. "But one thing is still missing: how did he get inside the Book Nook? There were no signs of forced entry."

"We think he could have had a key," Dink said. He shared his idea about the man stealing a set of keys when he left the Mark Twain party flyers.

Officer Fallon raised his eyebrows.

He took a sip of his tea. "A stolen key," he mumbled. "Possible, I guess."

Dink pointed to the drawing of the Mark Twain House on the flyer. "They're having a big party there tomorrow night," he said. "And I heard this guy talking about it on his cell phone. He might work there!"

"This is a good lead, kids," Officer Fallon said. "Officer Keene is out talking with the plumber, Amanda Dale. As soon as he gets back, we'll go visit Mark Twain's old home."

He copied the address from Dink's flyer—351 Farmington Avenue, Hartford, Connecticut. "I've always meant to see that place," he said. "I love his books."

The kids left the police station and walked to Main Street. The rain had stopped, but the sky was dark and a cool wind whipped up the street.

"I'm glad we told him," Ruth Rose

said. "Now the police have two good suspects: Amanda and the Mark Twain guy."

"I feel bad," Josh said. "If I hadn't made up that April Fools' Day trick to play on Mr. Paskey, his store wouldn't have gotten robbed."

"Josh, it's not your fault there are crooks in the world," Dink said.

"Besides, you never even got to tell him about the nickel," Ruth Rose said. "His coins got stolen before you had a chance."

"Yeah, I guess," Josh said. "Anyway, let's go to my house. I think my dad's baking critter cookies."

"What are critter cookies?" Dink asked.

"Dad has a bunch of metal cookie cutters shaped like animals," Josh said. "He can make elephants, lions, you name it."

Ten minutes later, they were kicking off their wet shoes in Josh's kitchen.

They hung their jackets on hooks. "Anybody home?" Josh yelled.

Pal, the family basset hound, came loping around the corner. Dink gave the dog a hug and got a wet slurp from Pal's tongue.

"Aha!" Josh said. He walked over to the kitchen table, where a plate of sand-

wiches and cookies waited, covered in aluminum foil. A note was taped on top, with SANDWICHES FIRST! written in his dad's handwriting.

Josh was pulling off the foil when the basement door burst open. Josh's dad stepped into the kitchen. Mr. Pinto was tall and thin and looked like Josh. "Freeze, cookie crooks!" he called out. "I caught you red-handed, and I'm calling Officer Fallon!"

"We just saw Officer Fallon, Dad," Josh said. He told his father all about Mr. Paskey's stolen coin collection as he and his friends ate their sandwiches.

"My goodness!" his father said. "Do they have any leads?"

"A couple," Josh said. They explained about Amanda and the guy who'd left Ellie's in such a hurry. Josh filled him in on the joke that he'd never gotten to play on Mr. Paskey.

"That's quite a trick," Josh's dad said.

"Can we take some cookies upstairs?" Josh asked his father.

"Sure. Bring a few up for the twins, too," he said. "I don't know what they're doing, but I hear strange noises from their room!"

"Where's Mom?" Josh asked.

"Yoga class," his father said. "Then food shopping for dinner."

Josh placed some of the cookies on a smaller plate. The three kids went up to Josh's room. Pal followed them up the stairs. His long ears made swishing noises as they dragged on the stair carpeting.

"Anyone want to play Monopoly?" Josh asked.

"Yeah, sure, if you want to get beat," Dink said.

"Beat by me!" Ruth Rose added.

Josh got the Monopoly game out of his closet, and they all sat on the floor.

He left the cookies on top of his desk, out of Pal's reach.

They each chose a piece for moving around the board while Ruth Rose divided up the money.

"Hey, what's this key for?" Dink asked. He was holding a silver key that looked as if it once opened a castle door.

"Oh, I lost one of the pieces," Josh said. "So Mom gave me that to use."

"Do you really think that guy we saw in Ellie's stole Mr. Paskey's key?" Ruth Rose asked Dink.

"I don't know," Dink said. "He could have, and it would explain how he got inside the Book Nook last night."

"Unless he has super abilities," Josh said in a whispery voice. "Maybe he's *Shadow Man*! He slips under doors to commit his crimes!"

Dink and Ruth Rose laughed. "Then why didn't Shadow Man leave the same way, under the door?" Ruth Rose asked. "Why climb out through the bathroom window?"

"Because he was carrying a heavy box of coins!" Josh said. "It wouldn't fit under the door."

Just then they heard a roar from the twins' room. The next thing they could hear was "PLEASE, MR. BEAR, DON'T GOBBLE ME UP!"

CHAPTER 10

"Come on," Josh said. Dink, Ruth Rose, and Pal followed him into the room Brian and Bradley shared. Toys, stuffed animals, games, and clothing were all over the floor.

Bradley was sitting on his bed, laughing into a pillow. "Please don't eat me, Mr. Bear. I'm a good boy!" he said. "You can eat Josh instead. He's a very, very bad boy!"

Dink grinned at Josh. "Bradley knows you," he said.

The twins had tacked a white sheet

so it hung from the ceiling. Brian was behind the sheet, standing in front of a flashlight. The flashlight cast Brian's shadow onto the sheet.

Brian was pretending to be a wild bear. He was standing on a chair to make himself look tall. He growled and waved his arms in the air. He wore a backpack to make his shadow appear bigger.

Dink stared at the shadow. A minute ago, when Josh was talking about Shadow Man, he'd had a thought, but it flew from his brain. Now, when he saw Brian's shadow, the thought came back.

"Guys, I just remembered!" Dink cried. "There was someone *else* in the Book Nook yesterday!"

"There was?" Ruth Rose asked. "Who?"

"I don't know," Dink said. "But when we were standing at the counter, I saw a reflection in the mirror. It was in the

shadows, so that's all I saw. Then it disappeared."

"So you think it was a fourth person?" Josh asked. "Besides Amanda, the delivery guy, and Mr. Blue Sneakers?"

"I think so," Dink said. "I forgot all about it till just now. Seeing Brian's shadow made me remember."

Brian walked out from behind the sheet. "Were you scared?" he asked his twin.

"You really looked like a bear with that backpack on," Bradley said.

Brian slipped out of the backpack and dropped it on his bed, where Ruth Rose was sitting. She stared at the backpack.

"Dink, I think I might know who the fourth person was!" she said.

"Who?" Dink asked.

"Remember when we first got to the Book Nook yesterday?" Ruth Rose asked.

Dink and Josh nodded.

"A woman was standing by the door," Ruth Rose went on. "She was reading that flyer about coin collecting, and then she walked into the store ahead of us. With a backpack on!"

"I *do* remember her!" Dink said. "But I didn't see her inside."

"I remember her, too," Josh said. "Her backpack had a yellow smiley face attached to one of the straps. I didn't see her inside the Book Nook, either."

"Dink, do you think you saw *her* reflection in the shadows?" Ruth Rose asked.

"It might have been, but then where did she go?" Dink asked. "Mr. Paskey locked up after the other three people left."

Josh giggled. "Shadow Man is back," he whispered. "He turns himself into a woman, then slips under the locked door!"

"There's no such thing as Shadow Man!" Bradley yelled.

Josh looked at the twins. "This room is a mess," he said. "I brought up some critter cookies. If you pick up all this stuff in one minute, you can have some."

Bradley and Brian tore around the room, grabbing clothes, animals, and toys off the floor. Josh said, "Ticktock, ticktock," as the boys raced around, throwing stuff into their closet and onto shelves. A minute later, the room looked much neater.

"Okay, good job," Josh said. "The cookies are in my room. And don't make another mess!"

The twins shot out of their room and disappeared down the hallway.

Dink watched as Josh pulled out the tacks and began folding the sheet.

"Dink? You look lost in space," Ruth Rose said.

"I'm trying to remember what was happening in the Book Nook when I saw that shadow," he said.

"I know what was happening," Josh said. "Mr. Paskey was showing us that coin book and the box holding his collection."

Dink stared at Josh. "Where's the book?" he asked.

"In my room," Josh said.

Dink turned and walked down the hall into Josh's room, with Josh and Ruth Rose right behind him.

The twins were sitting on Josh's bed with mouths full of cookies. The plate sat on the bed between them. It was empty.

"Dudes, you ate them all?" Josh yelled. "Three were for us!"

"You didn't say we couldn't!" Brian wailed.

Josh shook his head. "Go play somewhere," he said.

The twins tore out of the room, giggling.

Josh pulled the blue book from a shelf and handed it to Dink.

Dink found the page that described the three-million-dollar nickel. "Okay, we were all at the counter," he said to Josh and Ruth Rose. "Mr. Paskey told Amanda she could wash up in the bathroom. I think that's when I saw the shadowy reflection in the mirror. It was moving between some bookshelves."

"So it couldn't have been Amanda," Ruth Rose said. "She was in the bathroom."

"That's when Mr. Paskey showed us the picture of this nickel in the book," Josh added.

"No, wait a minute," Dink said. "Amanda left the Book Nook *before* Mr. Paskey gave you the book. I remember him locking the door behind her."

"Dink's right," Ruth Rose said. "Amanda left, then Mr. Paskey gave you the book and showed us his coin box."

Dink nodded. "So I think that woman with the backpack was standing in the shadows, listening," he said. "She probably heard Mr. Paskey when he told us the nickel was worth three million dollars."

"That's when she decided to steal it!" Ruth Rose exclaimed.

"Guys, Mr. Paskey was only showing us a *picture* of that nickel in the book," Josh said. "There was no real nickel."

"But the woman didn't *know* that," Dink said. "She couldn't see this book from where she was behind the bookshelves. When she heard Mr. Paskey say *This nickel is worth three million dollars,* she thought he was talking about a real nickel. She probably thought he had it right there, in his collection!"

"Which is why she stole the box!" Josh said.

"I'll bet she was hiding somewhere until Mr. Paskey went home," Ruth Rose added. "That's why we don't remember seeing her once we got inside the store."

"I've been thinking about that," Dink said. "She could've snuck down into the basement, waited for Mr. Paskey to leave, then come back up to steal the coins."

"This all makes sense now!" Josh said. "She smashed the case, grabbed the box, then climbed onto the toilet and hopped out through the bathroom window. Leaving wet footprints!"

"And disappeared," Ruth Rose said. "She could be anywhere."

"Don't be so sure," Dink said. Grinning at Josh, he tapped his forehead. "I have a *brilliant* idea!"

CHAPTER 11

"What is it?" Josh asked.

"Mr. Paskey collects old and rare coins because he loves it," Dink said. "It's his hobby."

"Yeah, because he's a noo-MIZ-muh-tist," Josh said.

Dink nodded at Josh. "But whoever stole his coin collection is probably just after the money the coins are worth," he continued.

Josh pulled the flyer about the Numismatic Society meeting from his pocket. "Maybe the crook plans to sell Mr. Paskey's coins at this meeting!" he said.

"That's what I was thinking," Ruth Rose said. She leaned closer and read the print. "It's today."

Dink closed his eyes. He pictured the woman with the backpack walking into the Book Nook. "She had to go right past the counter," he said. "She could've seen the flyers and picked one up, just like we did!"

Josh looked at the flyer again. "The meeting is on all day," he said. Then he grinned. "And they serve free refreshments!"

"It's at the library in West Hartford," Dink said, reading from the flyer. "On Main Street."

"West Hartford isn't very far from Green Lawn," Ruth Rose said. "About a twenty-minute bus ride."

Dink, Josh, and Ruth Rose looked at each other.

"Let's do it!" Ruth Rose said.

"I'll tell my dad we're going," Josh said. He raced out of the room.

"I'll text my mom and ask her to call yours, Dink," Ruth Rose said. She whipped out her cell phone and keyed in her message.

"I told her we'd be back in a few hours," she told Dink.

"Come on, you guys!" Josh yelled from downstairs.

Dink and Ruth Rose hurried down the stairs and into the kitchen. Josh was eating a lion-shaped cookie.

"Grab some for yourselves," he said to his friends.

Dink and Ruth Rose each took a critter cookie, and they headed out the door. The closest bus stop was in front of the Green Lawn Savings Bank, so they hiked down Main Street.

The rain and wind had stopped. Dink saw patches of blue sky over the bank. The clock out front said one o'clock.

"So when does this West Hartford bus come along?" Josh asked.

"I don't know," Ruth Rose said. "But I can find out."

She ran over to the elderly housing building and dashed up the front steps.

"What will we do if we find this woman?" Josh asked Dink. "I mean, we don't know if she really did steal Mr. Paskey's coins. The thief could still be Amanda or that guy sitting behind us in Ellie's yesterday."

"Or it could be none of them," Dink said. "But we have to try, for Mr. Paskey. Besides, don't you want to see all the money at this meeting?"

Josh grinned. "Yeah, especially now that I'm a noo-MIZ-muh-tist dude!"

Ruth Rose came back to them. "Every half hour," she said. "It'll say WEST HARTFORD CENTER on the front of the bus. It goes up Farmington Avenue and drops us near the library."

Fifteen minutes later, the bus came along. The kids clambered aboard.

"Oops, I forgot about money," Dink said. "I spent all mine on our hot chocolates."

"I have money," Ruth Rose said.

"Me too," Josh said. "I'll take care of you, Dink—like always!"

Josh and Ruth Rose dropped money into the coin box, and the kids found seats.

"How will we recognize this woman?" Ruth Rose whispered.

"Why are you whispering?" Josh asked.

"Because if she's also going to this Numismatic Society meeting," Ruth Rose said, "she could be on this bus!"

The kids looked around. They saw five men, two women, and four teenage boys.

One of the women was too large to fit in Mr. Paskey's tiny bathroom window.

The other one had white hair, and a cane was propped next to her.

"I don't think it was either of those women," Dink said. "The one we saw

yesterday was thin. I think she was tall.
That's all I remember."

"She had a black backpack," Ruth
Rose said.

"She was chewing flavored gum,"
Josh said.

Dink looked at him. "How do you
know that?" he asked.

"I smelled it," Josh said. "Wild cherry,
I think."

"Do you guys remember anything about her hair?" Ruth Rose asked.

"I'm pretty sure she had hair," said Josh.

Ruth Rose poked him. "I mean what color, short or long, straight or curly," she said.

"She might have been wearing a hat," Dink said. "It was about to rain, remember?"

Twenty minutes later, the driver called out, "West Hartford Center!"

The kids walked to the front of the bus. "Can you tell us where the library is?" Dink asked him.

The man pointed out the window. "Walk past the church, and it's the next building," he said. "Can't miss it. There's a statue of Noah Webster in front of the place."

They climbed down and started walking. "Who's Noah Webster?" Josh asked.

"He wrote a spelling book a long time ago," Dink said.

"Plus, he helped write the Merriam-Webster dictionary," Ruth Rose added. "You probably have one on your desk, Josh."

"So why'd they name this library after him?" Josh asked as they approached a large brick church on the left.

"I think he lived in West Hartford," Dink said. "I'll bet we could find his house around here someplace."

"I see Noah Webster!" Ruth Rose said.

About a hundred feet ahead of them stood a statue. It was around fifteen feet tall, and the white marble gleamed when the sun shone through the clouds. Noah Webster wore a long robe and a serious expression on his face.

"He looks like he had a headache the day the sculptor carved this," Josh said. "Probably from memorizing all those words in his dictionary."

"You're so funny," Dink said. "Come on, let's go find the noo-MIZ-muh-tist meeting!"

CHAPTER 12

The kids shoved open a thick door and entered the library. Straight ahead was a long counter where two men and a woman sorted and checked out books. Behind them was a computer room where a bunch of people sat at keyboards.

Dink looked to see if the woman they were after was in there. No one seemed familiar.

One of the men behind the counter smiled at the kids. "The children's room is downstairs," he said, pointing toward a set of stairs.

"We're looking for the numismatic meeting," Ruth Rose said.

"That's down there, too," the man said. "Take a left at the bottom of the stairs. They're in the Nutmeg Room."

Dink, Josh, and Ruth Rose headed for the stairs. "What's nutmeg?" Josh asked as they walked down.

"I think it's a kind of spice," Ruth Rose said. "My grandmother puts it in her Christmas pudding."

"You get it from a nut," Dink added.

Josh giggled.

They turned left at the bottom of the stairs. The first thing Dink saw was a policeman. He had wide shoulders and was a lot taller than Officer Fallon and Officer Keene. His name tag said SGT. O. RICH.

Dink walked over and asked Officer Rich if he knew where the Nutmeg Room was.

"Right here," the officer said. He

stepped aside, revealing a door. Taped to it was a flyer like the one in Josh's pocket.

"Can we go in?" Ruth Rose asked.

"Sure," the officer said. He opened the door and held it as the kids walked into the room. "Have fun, but no touching the money!"

The Nutmeg Room was huge and filled with people. Along three walls, Dink could see tables draped with green cloths. Most of the tables held glass cases where coins and bills were displayed. The people standing behind the tables wore tags on lanyards around their necks. The tags had each person's name, then NUMISMATIC SOCIETY.

"Welcome!" a cheery voice said.

Just inside the door was a smaller table. A man and woman sat there to greet people as they came in. A microphone stood on the table, next to a laptop. The woman was smiling at the three kids.

"Would you like a map of the room?" she asked. "This will help you find the dealers."

"Thank you," Dink said, taking a sheet that showed the room's layout. The tables were numbered. "Can you tell us which dealer buys old coins?"

The woman laughed. "They all do, dear," she said. "All the dealers come here to buy and sell."

Some new people came through the door, so the kids moved out of the way.

"I don't see any free food," Josh said, standing on tiptoes. "Just a jillion people looking at coins."

Dink showed Josh the sheet of paper. "The food is on table seventeen," he said.

"Does anyone see that woman from yesterday?" Ruth Rose asked.

"If she's in this room, we'll never find her," Josh said. "There are a lot of women

WELCOME, NUMISMATIC SOCIETY
EXIT

here. She could be any one of them, if she's here at all. She might not have picked up a flyer."

"If she's not here, at least we tried," Ruth Rose said. "But even if she didn't get a flyer, she was reading the one taped to Mr. Paskey's window when we saw her at the Book Nook."

"But we don't know if she *is* the thief," Josh said.

"Let's split up," Dink suggested. "Keep your eye out for someone skinny enough to crawl through Mr. Paskey's bathroom window."

"Wouldn't it be great if she was here and she was carrying Mr. Paskey's wooden box?" Ruth Rose whispered.

"I don't think she'd want to be seen with it," Dink said. "She might have gotten rid of the box and just brought the coins with her."

"If she's even here," Josh repeated.

"I know," Dink said. "But we *are* here, so let's look around." He pointed at a table where a plump man stood next to a sign that said CHUCK'S RARE COINS. It was table number one. "Let's look around and meet back at this table in about ten minutes."

Suddenly they heard a cheery voice over a hidden speaker: *"Ladies and gentlemen, just a few reminders: We close our door at four o'clock today. Smoking is not allowed in this building. And please stop at our food table for a free snack and beverage!"*

Dink turned around. The voice came from the woman who had greeted them.

"Now we're talking!" Josh said. "See you guys in ten minutes."

Dink said to Ruth Rose, "Okay, why don't we each check out one side of the room? The food is in the back, so Josh will look around there."

"I wish I knew what she looked like," Ruth Rose said. "Yesterday we only saw her from behind."

Dink and Ruth Rose went their separate ways. Dink strolled past several green-topped tables, hoping to spot a skinny woman who looked familiar. He noticed one thin woman standing at a table. When he got closer, Dink realized it was really a thin man. He kept walking.

Dink bumped into Josh at the end of the room. Josh was munching something and wiping his fingers on a paper napkin.

"Did you see her?" Dink asked his friend. "Or were your eyes closed while you enjoyed your treat?"

Josh laughed. "I kept both eyes open, but I didn't see anyone who looked like the woman we saw yesterday," he said. "There are just too many people!"

"Come on, let's keep moving," Dink said. "Ruth Rose is on the other side of the room. Maybe she'll have better luck."

But when the three kids met at the Chuck's Rare Coins table, no one had spotted their quarry.

Just then another announcement came over the loudspeaker: *"Hello again, folks. I have a gentleman here who has misplaced his little boy. Oliver Sidney, if you can hear my voice, please come to the front. Your daddy is waiting for you!"*

Everyone looked toward the front. The woman on the microphone was standing next to a worried-looking man. That was when Dink saw a tall, thin woman enter the room. She picked up a floor plan from the table and began studying it. The strap of a backpack was slung over the woman's shoulder.

"I think I see her!" Dink whispered to Josh and Ruth Rose.

Just then a small boy came running out of the crowd. "I'm Oliver!" he cried. "Hi, Daddy!"

Everyone began clapping as the boy leaped into his father's arms.

When Dink tried to spot the woman again, she was gone.

CHAPTER 13

"You saw her?" Josh asked. "Where was she?"

Dink pointed. "She came in the door when that little kid ran up to his father," he said. "I took my eyes off her for two seconds, and she had disappeared!"

"Do you think she recognized us and left the room?" Ruth Rose asked.

"I doubt it," Dink said. "Too many tall people standing between us."

Josh glanced around the room. "So she must be in here somewhere," he whispered. "What was she wearing?"

"She had that black backpack," Dink said. "And jeans, I think. Oh, and a light-blue jacket with a hood."

"Did you see her hair?" Ruth Rose asked.

Dink grinned at Ruth Rose. "She had hair," he said.

"Okay, here's the plan," Josh said, taking charge. "We move toward the front together. Dink, you check everyone on the right. Ruth Rose, keep your eyes on the left. I'll be front man."

"But what if she sees us before we see her?" Ruth Rose asked. "If she recognized us from the Book Nook, she'd take off!"

"We don't have a choice," Dink said. "Besides, she'll be checking out the coins. Plus, she doesn't know that anyone is looking for her."

The kids moved slowly toward the front of the room. Their eyes fell on every woman, looking for a backpack and a blue jacket.

"Dude, there are a lot of women in blue jackets," Josh muttered.

"This was light blue," Dink said. "Sky blue."

Five minutes later, Ruth Rose put out her hands and stopped the boys from walking any farther. "There she is," she whispered.

"That's the woman I saw come in," Dink said quietly.

The woman was fifteen feet in front of them. She was leaning over a table where coins were on display. She had tied her jacket sleeves around her waist.

"Are you sure it's the woman from yesterday?" Josh asked Dink.

"Positive," Dink said. "Look at the straps on her backpack. One of them has a yellow smiley face attached to it."

"I remember that!" Ruth Rose said.

They inched closer, keeping other people between them and the woman. The smiley face was clearly visible. Dink knew this was the woman who had entered the Book Nook yesterday. But did she steal Mr. Paskey's coin collection?

"I'd give anything to know what's in her backpack," Ruth Rose said.

"Me too," Dink said. He glanced at

Josh. "Where's Shadow Man when we need him?"

"Shadow Man is on vacation," Josh said. "But his friend Invisible Man is taking his place." He pulled his hood up over his red hair. "She'll never see me!"

"What are you going to do?" Dink asked.

"Watch," Josh said. Then he walked away and crept up behind the woman.

He stood next to her, pretending to be looking at the coins on the table.

Dink and Ruth Rose watched Josh place his hand on the woman's backpack. They watched his fingers give it a squeeze.

"I'm going to faint," Dink whispered.

"Me first," Ruth Rose said.

Josh headed back toward Dink and Ruth Rose. He held two thumbs up in the air.

"Whatever she's got in there is square and hard," Josh said. "It could be Mr. Paskey's wooden box."

"Could also be books," Dink said. He kept his eye on the woman as she moved to another dealer.

"Or a laptop," Ruth Rose said.

Josh grinned. "Maybe it's a pizza!" he said.

"How do we find out?" Ruth Rose asked.

"Can Invisible Man turn himself into a mouse?" Dink asked Josh. "A mouse could crawl right inside the backpack!"

"Very funny, bunny," Josh said.

"We have to just keep following her," Ruth Rose said. "Maybe she'll show the coins to one of these dealers."

The woman moved slowly around the room, stopping at several tables. She seemed to be talking to the dealers, but the kids couldn't hear what was being said. She never opened her backpack.

"If she decides to leave, we can't stop her!" Dink said.

"Oh yeah?" Ruth Rose said. "Meet me by the door!"

Dink and Josh watched Ruth Rose wiggle through the crowd. They followed her at a distance, then lost sight of her.

"What's Ruth Rose doing?" Dink asked Josh. "Can you see her?"

"No, but if I know Ruth Rose, she'll probably tackle that woman," Josh said.

Dink and Josh moved slowly through the crowd, toward the entrance.

"I see Ruth Rose!" Dink said. "She's near the door, talking to that lady with the microphone."

"Uh-oh," Josh said.

A few seconds later, the loudspeaker crackled. Then a voice spoke: *"Hello again, folks. I have a young lady here who has misplaced her backpack. She says her friend's coin collection is inside, in a special carved wooden box. If you—"*

Dink and Josh watched Ruth Rose say something else to the microphone lady.

"The backpack has a yellow smiley face on one of the straps. If anyone sees the backpack, please let us know immediately!"

Dink was holding his breath. Josh

was holding Dink's arm. The room got even noisier as people talked to each other. Then the room grew quiet again.

"Over here!" a loud voice called out.

Dink and Josh turned to look where everyone else was looking. An empty space had opened in the crowd. In the middle of the space stood the woman with the sky-blue jacket tied around her waist.

Dangling from one hand was the backpack. Everyone could see the smiley face pin.

CHAPTER 14

To Dink, it seemed as if the entire crowd in the Nutmeg Room was playing statues. Everyone stood frozen in place, staring at the woman with the backpack.

Then came the friendly voice over the loudspeaker: *"Oh, lovely, you've found the backpack! Please bring it to the front and make this young lady very happy!"*

The crowd opened up, making a path for the woman toward the front of the room.

The woman hesitated, then started to walk. Her face was pink, but she managed a little smile. She held the backpack tight against her chest, grasping the straps with both hands.

"Come on!" Dink said. He and Josh raced around the crowd and got to the lady with the microphone first. Ruth Rose was standing there, watching the woman come closer.

She stopped walking when she was about halfway to the microphone lady.

"Is that your backpack, dear?" the lady at the table asked Ruth Rose.

"It looks like mine," Ruth Rose said.

"I'm afraid you're mistaken," said the woman carrying it. "This is my backpack. I bought it last year at Books 'n' Things in Hartford."

"That's where I got mine, too!" Ruth Rose said. "My friend's coin collection is in it. The coins are in a pretty wooden box with carvings all over it."

"Well, why don't we ask this nice

woman if she'd mind opening the backpack for us," the other lady said. "That
will clear up the confusion."

By now everyone in the Nutmeg
Room had stopped talking and was
watching and listening.

Suddenly the woman flung the back-pack. It knocked over the microphone, bounced off the table, and landed at Ruth Rose's feet. The woman bolted for the door just as everyone started yelling, "Stop her! Stop her!"

Before the woman could reach the door, it opened. She ran right into the long arms of Officer Rich. "What's your rush, miss?" the cop asked.

The lady at the table picked up her microphone. Ruth Rose grabbed the backpack and held on tight.

"Go ahead," the lady said. "Open it, dear."

Ruth Rose opened the pack, grinned, and pulled out Mr. Paskey's carved box.

"Is this it?" the woman asked.

"Yes!" said Ruth Rose. "It belongs to my friend Mr. Paskey. He owns the Book Nook in Green Lawn."

"My goodness!" the lady said. She pulled out a cell phone. "Why don't we call him and let him know his coin collection is safe?"

She looked up the Book Nook and typed the number into her phone. "It's ringing," she said. "Hello, is this Mr.

Paskey? This is Lorraine Landers at the Numismatic Society. I believe I have some good news for you!"

She handed the phone to Ruth Rose, who told him they had found the thief and his coin collection. "We'll bring it to the Book Nook," she added.

Officer Rich called for backup, and two other officers showed up. They escorted the woman in the blue jacket from the room.

"How are we getting home?" Josh asked. "We don't know when the next bus for Green Lawn comes."

Officer Rich stepped forward. "I guess I can take you kids home," he said. "I'll tell my captain I'm guarding this valuable coin collection!"

The kids thanked the microphone lady.

"The pleasure was all mine, dears!" she said. "This was the most exciting meeting the Numismatic Society has ever had!"

Dink, Josh, and Ruth Rose followed Officer Rich to his cruiser.

"Anyone want to sit up front with me?" he asked.

"I do!" Josh yelped.

Officer Rich smiled. "Climb in, then," he said. "But don't touch any buttons or knobs!"

While they were heading for Green Lawn, Officer Rich made a call and found out the thief's name. He called Officer Fallon to let him know what was going on.

Twenty minutes later, the cruiser stopped in front of the Book Nook. The kids hopped out and thanked Officer Rich for the ride. Ruth Rose was carrying the carved wooden box in her arms like a baby.

"No problem," the officer said. "When you kids grow up, maybe you'd like to join the police force!"

"Thanks, but I want to be a writer," Dink said.

"And I'm going to be president!" Ruth Rose added.

Josh grinned. "Can I be a police officer and an artist and a noo-MIZ-muh-tist?"

Officer Rich laughed as he pulled away and aimed his cruiser up Main Street.

Inside the Book Nook, the kids found Officer Fallon talking with Mr. Paskey.

"Well, here are the three intrepid sleuths!" Officer Fallon said. "But I wish you'd told me your plans."

"You were busy looking for that guy who ran out of Ellie's," Ruth Rose said.

"And we found him where he works, at the Mark Twain House," Officer Fallon said. "His name is Ron Ronald, and he's in charge of this big celebration they have every April for Mark Twain. He had a perfect alibi for the night the coin box was taken."

"Where was he?" Dink asked.

"In the hospital!" Officer Fallon said. "Mr. Ronald is allergic to nuts, and there were nuts in the ice cream he ordered at Ellie's. That's why he charged out of the diner so fast. He drove right to the emergency room."

"But if he knew he was allergic, why did he get ice cream with nuts in it?" Dink asked.

"I asked him the same question," Officer Fallon said. "It seems Mr. Ronald had taken his glasses off as he walked into Ellie's. He didn't see the sign that said THESE FOUR FLAVORS CONTAIN NUTS, and he ordered one of them."

"So that's why he didn't finish eating it," Josh said.

"Is Ron Ronald going to be all right?" Ruth Rose asked.

"His doc told me he'll be fine soon," Officer Fallon said. "And Ellie is going to bring him a free gallon of his favorite flavor when he's feeling better. Without nuts!"

"Lucky guy!" Josh said.

"And we did find Amanda Dale's fingerprints in the bathroom," Officer Fallon went on, "but only on the water faucets and sink. She never touched that window."

Ruth Rose placed Mr. Paskey's wooden box on the counter. "Maybe you should make sure everything is still in it," she said.

Mr. Paskey opened the box lid and did a quick check of all the coins. "Nothing is missing," he said.

"Good thing you kids caught the thief before she sold anything," Officer Fallon said. "Her name is Pam Sprat. She confessed to hiding in the basement here and stealing the box after Mr.

Paskey went home. *Her* fingerprints are all over the bathroom window."

"Is she in jail?" Josh asked.

Officer Fallon nodded. "Yup," he said. "Turns out Ms. Sprat is quite the thief. We matched her prints to at least three other break-ins. She had burglar tools in her backpack, along with a can of spray paint! You kids deserve a reward for catching her!"

Mr. Paskey opened a drawer and pulled out three gift cards. He handed one to each kid. "Free ice cream from Ellie's for one year!" he said.

Josh closed one eye and looked at Mr. Paskey with the other. "Is this another April Fools' Day joke?" he asked.

Mr. Paskey grinned. "Why, Joshua, how can you accuse me?" he asked. "I would never play an April Fools' trick on April second!"

DID YOU FIND THE
SECRET MESSAGE
HIDDEN IN THIS BOOK?

If you *don't* want
to know the answer,
don't look at the bottom
of this page!

Answer:
WILL YOU FIND THE NEXT RARE COIN?

HAVE YOU READ ALL THE BOOKS IN THE

A to Z Mysteries®

SERIES?

Help Dink, Josh, and Ruth Rose . . .

. . . solve
mysteries
from A to Z!

A TO Z MYSTERIES® fans, check out Ron Roy's other great mystery series!

Capital Mysteries

#1: Who Cloned the President?
#2: Kidnapped at the Capital
#3: The Skeleton in the Smithsonian
#4: A Spy in the White House
#5: Who Broke Lincoln's Thumb?
#6: Fireworks at the FBI
#7: Trouble at the Treasury
#8: Mystery at the Washington Monument
#9: A Thief at the National Zoo
#10: The Election-Day Disaster
#11: The Secret at Jefferson's Mansion
#12: The Ghost at Camp David
#13: Trapped on the D.C. Train!
#14: Turkey Trouble on the National Mall

Calendar Mysteries

January Joker
February Friend
March Mischief
April Adventure
May Magic
June Jam
July Jitters
August Acrobat
September Sneakers
October Ogre
November Night
December Dog
New Year's Eve Thieves

If you like **A TO Z MYSTERIES**®, take a swing at

BALLPARK® Mysteries